for Elena, Luce and Nina

Copyright © 1998 by Fulvio Testa
The rights of Fulvio Testa to be identified as the author and illustrator of this work have been asserted by him in accordance
with the Copyright, Designs and Patents Act, 1988.
First published in Great Britain in 1998 by Andersen Press Ltd., 20 Vauxhall Bridge Road, London SW1V 2SA. Published in
Australia by Random House Australia Pty., 20 Alfred Street, Milsons Point, Sydney, NSW 2061. All rights reserved.
Colour separated by Fotoriproduzioni Grafiche, Verona. Printed and bound in Italy by Grafiche AZ, Verona.

10   9   8   7   6   5   4   3   2   1

British Library Cataloguing in Publication Data available.
ISBN 0 86264 799 1

This book has been printed on acid-free paper

CAT AND MOUSE
AND
SOMETHING TO DO

by Fulvio Testa

Ⓐ

Andersen Press · London

Why are you bored?
Is there nothing to do?
What are you thinking?

Give us a clue . . .

You are looking for something.
Will it be there?

That looks quite heavy.
You'd better take care.

First you went up.
Now you come down.
What will you do
With the things that you've found?

You're in the kitchen.
What do you need?
Perhaps it's the cat
That you ought to feed?

You missed the sardines.
The cat missed them too...
But *he's* found something,

And so have you!